To my Boulder writing friends, with thanks and love:

Cathy Conery, Mary DeLancy, Elaine Long, Joyce Gellhorn,
Susan Hellie, Pat Maslowski, Marge Warsavage,
Lindsay Calhoun

Marie Desjardin, Claire Martin, Claudia Mills,
Leslie O'Kane, Phyllis Perry,
Ina Robbins, Elizabeth Wrenn

And with special thanks
to Joseph Kurtz, for helping me
when I lost my way
A. W. N.

To my sister,
Kimberly Larson,
With love,
Steph

Dear Whiskers

Hannah

by Ann Whitehead Nagda

illustrated by

Stephanie Roth

A
**LITTLE
APPLE**
PAPERBACK

SCHOLASTIC INC.
New York   Toronto   London   Auckland   Sydney
Mexico City   New Delhi   Hong Kong   Buenos Aires

With special thanks to Rima Hassan
at the Information Office at the Royal Embassy
of Saudi Arabia for her help.

ISBN 0-439-37589-4

All rights reserved. Published by Scholastic Inc., 555 Broadway, New York, NY 10012,
by arrangement with Holiday House, Inc. SCHOLASTIC and associated logos are
trademarks and/or registered trademarks of Scholastic Inc.

12 11 10 9 8 7 6 5 4 3   2 3 4 5 6 7/ 0

Printed in the U.S.A.   40

First Scholastic printing, March 2002

Chapter 1

Dear Sameera,
I am a mouse.
I live in your desk.

Jenny put down her pencil. She didn't know what else to write. It was bad enough to have to write a letter, but to pretend to be a mouse . . . That was silly.

Beside her, Susan was writing and writing. Susan had long blond hair and bright pink polish on her fingernails. She was the best writer in the class.

"I thought Mrs. Steele said a short letter," Jenny whispered.

Susan smiled, but kept on writing.

Kevin sat on Jenny's other side. He hadn't written anything yet. He was wearing his favorite snake shirt. It had a big snake with a flicking tongue that rose out of his shirt pocket. Another snake was coiled by his stomach. The shirt made Jenny shiver. She didn't like snakes much. She didn't like Kevin much, either.

Jenny twisted her earring. Her ear was itchy. She took the earring off.

"You've got a hole in your ear," Richard whispered from the desk behind her. Jenny turned around and he smirked.

"You've got a hole in your head," Jenny whispered back. He also had holes in his jeans, and the sole of one shoe flapped when he walked. Jenny liked Richard, even though he teased her sometimes.

Jenny chewed on her pencil. Mrs. Steele, their teacher, had listed the five parts of a letter on the blackboard.

First, there was the date. Uh-oh. Jenny had forgotten that. She quickly wrote "October 9" at the top of the paper.

Next was the greeting. She had that. It was "Dear Sameera." Whoever that was. Some shrimpy second grader with a funny name. They had all drawn names from a box. Susan had picked a boy named Daniel. Richard had picked a boy named

Eric. Kevin had groaned because he picked a girl. Only Jenny had picked a kid with a weird name. She didn't even know if the kid was a boy or a girl.

Jenny looked at the board again. The body of the letter came next. A dead body. Jenny could write a letter with a dead body. She could say, "I am a dead mouse. Here is my body." She started to giggle.

Susan frowned at her. Susan had finally stopped writing. Susan's letter must have a hundred sentences. Jenny's only had two. She raised her hand.

"Yes, Jenny," said Mrs. Steele.

"Are two sentences enough for the body?"

"Four or five sentences would be better. We want to give the second graders lots of practice reading."

Why did her whole fourth-grade class have to pretend to be mice? Jenny wondered. She would rather be something else. "I am an elephant," she could write. "I stomp on your desk." She started to giggle again.

Mrs. Steele walked by. She was wearing her picnic-table dress. It was red and white just like the tablecloth Jenny's mother used in summer. Mrs. Steele touched Jenny's arm. "You can do it," she said encouragingly.

Jenny sighed and picked up her pencil again. What else could she write about? Her stomach grumbled. Food. Of course. "I am often hungry," she wrote. "I eat the crumbs from your lunch."

There. She had four sentences. But Susan had more. Thousands more.

Mrs. Steele stopped by Susan's desk. "Good work, Susan," she said.

Jenny chewed on her eraser. A piece came off in her mouth and she spit it out. If she were a mouse, what would she like to eat? Certainly not erasers. Jenny wrote, "I really like to eat chocolate brownies. They taste better than bread crumbs."

There. That was enough for the body, dead or alive.

She looked at the board again. The last items in a letter were the complimentary close and the signature. That really meant you signed your name after you wrote, "Sincerely." She hadn't decided on a name for her mouse. Susan had signed her name "Pepper Jack." That was dumb. Jack was a boy's name.

"Pepper Jack is a funny name," said Jenny.

"It's a kind of cheese—Monterey Jack cheese with peppers in it," explained Susan. "Haven't you ever had any?"

Jenny shook her head.

She turned around and looked at Richard's paper. He had signed his name "White Mouse."

Jenny drew a picture of a mouse at the bottom of her letter. She gave her mouse a pointy nose, two beady eyes, two round ears, a long skinny tail, and whiskers. And she signed her letter, "Sincerely, Wiskers."

"'Whiskers' should have an 'h' in it," whispered Susan.

"What?" said Jenny.

"W-H-I-S-K-E-R-S," said Susan, spelling it out slowly.

Jenny erased the mouse's name, almost tearing the paper. Then she wrote it correctly, pressing so hard with her pencil that the point broke off.

Chapter 2

It was Thursday. Mrs. Steele was wearing her astronaut dress. It was sparkly gray with a zipper down the front and a shiny silver belt.

Mrs. Steele had a stack of papers in her hand. "The second graders have written letters back to their mice," she said.

It had taken the second graders three days to write their letters. Jenny wondered how long the letters were. You could write a lot in three days. But maybe not if you were a second grader.

"Let's read the first few letters out loud," said Mrs. Steele.

Jenny groaned. She hated reading in front of the class.

"The first letter is for White Mouse. Who is that?"

Without even turning around, Jenny knew Richard was waving his arm back and forth. She could feel the air moving.

"Richard," said Mrs. Steele. "Come up front and read your letter."

Richard walked quickly to the front of the room. His shoe went *flap, flap, flap*. It sounded like someone using a flyswatter over and over. Mrs. Steele handed him the letter.

"Dear White Mouse,
    I like mouses. Whar in my desk do you live?
        Sincerely,
        Eric"

"That's a nice letter," said Mrs. Steele. "And now you have something to write back. You can describe where you live in Eric's desk."

"You mean we have to write *another* letter?" Richard asked.

"Oh, yes," said Mrs. Steele. "We're going to write lots of letters."

Richard looked as if someone had just punched him in the stomach. Jenny knew how he felt. She didn't like writing these dumb letters, either.

Mrs. Steele picked up the next letter.

Jenny held her breath. Please, don't let it be for Whiskers, she thought.

"Who is Pepper Jack?" said Mrs. Steele. "That's a clever name."

Susan pranced to the front of the room. Before she read, she pushed a long blond strand of her hair behind her ear. She cleared her throat. She looked around to make sure everyone was paying attention. Finally she read her letter.

"Dear Pepper Jack,
    I am happy to have a frend living in my desk.
Do you have any brothers or sisters?
They can live in my desk, too.
There is room for everyone.
I rily like rodints.
        Sincerely,
        Daniel"

Everyone laughed. Susan smiled again. She was wearing a pink blouse that looked new and rosebud earrings.

"In her next letter, Susan can tell Daniel about the mouse family," said Mrs. Steele.

Susan didn't need any help from the teacher. She never had any trouble thinking of things to write.

"My student wrote five sentences," Susan said proudly. "Next time I will tell him to write even more."

Mrs. Steele picked up another letter. The mouse's name was Smelly. Kevin went up front and read his letter. It was very short. It said, "Mice are nice. Mice are white. They have long tails."

Jenny hoped Mrs. Steele was finished with read-aloud time. But she picked up the next letter.

"This is fun," said Mrs. Steele. "Let's share a few more letters. Who is Whiskers?"

Jenny walked slowly to the front of the class and took the letter from Mrs. Steele. She hoped she wouldn't stumble over any words. She took a deep breath.

"Dear Whiskers," Jenny read in a loud, clear voice. "No mouse." She stopped. The handwriting was terrible. She squinted her eyes. "In desk," she read. "No mouse in desk?" she said again, her voice

trembling. She gulped. The letter was terrible. Jenny wanted to run out of the room and hide. Her student hadn't even written a complete sentence. It didn't have a verb. Jenny could barely read the last two words. "Sincerely, Sameera," she mumbled.

"Oh, dear," said Mrs. Steele. "Can you think of something nice to write back to her? Something that will convince her to play along?"

Jenny chewed her lip. She couldn't think of anything at all.

"What's the kid's name?" asked Kevin. "Smear-a? Like smear-a the bug on the window?"

Mrs. Steele gave Kevin a very stern look. "It's not nice to make fun of someone's name. You know that. Sameera is a new little girl in our school."

Jenny knew Kevin was being mean as usual. She knew it wasn't nice to make fun of someone, but right now she felt like making fun of Sameera.

"You could make your mouse do something funny," said Mary. She and Susan were good friends.

"Yes," said Mrs. Steele. "That might work. Any other ideas?"

Richard raised his hand. "We have mice in our pantry sometimes. They leave their doo-doos all over. That's how we know they're around. You could leave doo-doos in the kid's desk."

Everyone laughed. Everyone except Mrs. Steele.

"You could tell Sameera that make-believe is fun," said Susan.

"Yes," said Mrs. Steele. "I think that would be a good thing to write."

Jenny walked back to her seat. She smiled at Richard. She liked his idea much better than Susan's.

Chapter 3

Dear Sameera,
    Make-believe is fun. Pretend
there is a mouse in your desk.

    This wasn't the letter Jenny wanted to write.
This was Susan's idea. Jenny took out another
sheet of paper. She put a stack of books next to her
paper, so Susan couldn't read what she was writing.

Dear Sameera,
    I don't like writing letters.
I'm not very good at it.
But my teacher says I have to.
I had to read your first letter
to the class.
It made me
feel awful.

Jenny looked at Mrs. Steele. She was correcting math papers. Her teacher had brown curly hair and a nice smile. Jenny wanted Mrs. Steele to say, "Good work," to her someday just like she said it to Susan.

Jenny reread both letters. She put her real, longer letter inside her desk. She would send her "Susan" letter to Sameera. But it was only two sentences.

Jenny tried to think of something else to write. She looked over at Susan. Susan was staring out the window. A dog ran down the sidewalk outside.

Jenny pictured herself running beside the dog. If she were a real mouse, she could ride on the dog's back, holding on to its collar. If she were a real mouse, she wouldn't have to write silly letters.

Jenny leaned over and read Susan's letter. "I have two brothers and three sisters," Susan had written. "My two brothers live in the art supply closet. They make their nests from colored paper."

Susan was so clever. Jenny pictured piles of red and blue and yellow paper torn into little pieces.

Susan looked over at Jenny suddenly. Jenny sat up straight. Her heart pounded. She didn't want Susan to think she was copying. She pretended she was writing.

Jenny sighed. She could write that she had four brothers. That would be different from Susan. But where could they live? Maybe in the teachers' lounge. Jenny had always wondered what the teachers did in there. She could smell fresh coffee. She knew it had comfortable chairs. She had peered through the open door on the way to music several times. Jenny wondered if mice liked coffee. She finished her letter. It said:

Dear Sameera,
    Make-believe is fun. Pretend

there is a mouse in your desk.
Pretend that this mouse has
four brothers who live in the
teachers' lounge. The four
brothers drink the teachers'
coffee. It isn't good for young
mice to drink coffee, but they
do it anyway.

Sincerely,
Whiskers

Chapter 4

The next time Mrs. Steele handed back letters, she was wearing her admiral outfit. It was black with shiny gold buttons down the front and on the shoulders.

Jenny wasn't sure she wanted another letter from Sameera. She wondered if Susan's idea had worked. Would Sameera be willing to pretend now?

This time Mrs. Steele was just calling out mouse names, then handing back the letters. She wasn't making anyone read. Not yet. Jenny held her breath. The pile of letters got smaller and smaller. Had Sameera written anything at all?

Mrs. Steele walked to the front of the room. Her hands were empty. Jenny didn't get a letter. She felt like a loser. Her last letter didn't work.

Sameera hated her. Should Jenny raise her hand and tell Mrs. Steele? But then everyone in the class would know that her pen pal hated her. She didn't know what to do. Mrs. Steele asked for volunteers to read their letters.

Jenny looked down at her empty desk. She reached inside her desk and pulled out some papers. Susan looked at her. Jenny took the math paper on top of the pile and moved it to the bottom.

Susan wanted to read her letter. Jenny wasn't surprised. Susan cleared her throat, pawed the ground with her shiny black shoe, and started to read. Her second grader had no trouble with pretending.

"Dear Pepper Jack,
    What do you look like?
What do you do all day?
One of my frends has a rat.
The rat's name is Ratface.
Do you like rats? I like Swiss
chese better then American.
Witch one do you like.
        Sincerely,
        Daniel"

"Daniel is writing longer letters," said Susan smugly. "And his letters are so informative. I'm helping him."

Jenny felt like pounding the desk and screaming.

Next, Kevin shuffled to the front of the room and read his letter.

"Dear Smelly,
    Mice are nice.
Mice eat cheese.
I think."

Everyone laughed. Kevin shrugged and shuffled back to his seat. Jenny was glad his pen pal wasn't writing long, informative letters. Whatever that meant. She leaned over and looked at Daniel's letter. "Your pen pal doesn't spell very well," she told Susan.

"Students in second grade are supposed to use invented spelling," said Susan. "Daniel invents very well."

At lunch recess, Jenny sat on a swing and watched some girls play on the merry-go-round. They were small enough to be second graders. They were all laughing. Jenny couldn't imagine Sameera laughing. She must not be one of those girls. Some boys played soccer on the grass nearby. A little girl with black hair ran over and grabbed the ball. "You don't know how to play," said a short, skinny boy as he grabbed the ball back.

The black-haired girl yelled something strange before she walked away. But lots of kids were yelling, so maybe Jenny didn't hear it right. The little girl sat on a bench and kicked the dirt with her foot.

Jenny went inside early so that she could talk to Mrs. Steele. Alone. She didn't want to talk about not getting a letter in front of the class. Especially not in front of Susan.

She stood quietly beside Mrs. Steele's desk.

"Yes, Jenny?" said Mrs. Steele, looking up from a book. She stood up.

"I didn't get a letter today," said Jenny.

"Oh," said Mrs. Steele. "Maybe your pen pal is sick."

"Maybe she moved away," said Jenny. "Far away to the North Pole or someplace like that."

Mrs. Steele looked surprised. "Maybe," she said. "I'll write a note to Miss Murphy and find out what happened." Mrs. Steele took a notebook from her

desk drawer and started to write. "What is your pen pal's name?"

"Sameera," said Jenny.

"Oh, I remember," said Mrs. Steele. "Your first letter from Sameera was very short."

"Yes," Jenny agreed, "and it was . . ." She hesitated. She wanted to say "awful."

"It was disappointing, wasn't it?" said Mrs. Steele softly.

"Yes," said Jenny. She loved her teacher. She was the best teacher in the whole world. "Do you think I could have a new pen pal? Could you ask Miss Murphy?"

"Let's find out about Sameera first," said Mrs. Steele. She handed the note to Jenny. "Do you know where the second-grade classroom is?"

"Yes," said Jenny. She felt happy as she left the room. She walked down the hallway and wondered what Mrs. Steele had said in the note. She looked down at it. Mrs. Steele had written:

Dear Shirley,

I am sending Jenny to see you. Her pen pal is Sameera. Jenny has been working very hard on her letter writing. The first letter from Sameera was disappointing and there was no second letter at all. Maybe if you intro-

duced Sameera to Jenny, she would be more willing to correspond. Otherwise, the mouse letters are a great success. Call me later.

Marge

Jenny looked over her teacher's letter again. She noticed that Mrs. Steele had forgotten the date and the complimentary close.

Jenny folded the letter and entered the second-grade classroom. The children were just coming in from recess. "Hang up your coats," said Miss Murphy, "and then come and sit down on the rug." Two boys got into a shoving match by the coat closet. "Eric and Daniel, stop that!" she said sharply. "Come and sit down quickly and quietly. I'm going to read a story."

Miss Murphy noticed Jenny standing in the doorway. "May I help you?" she said wearily.

Jenny held out the letter from her teacher. Miss Murphy read it while her students found seats on the rug. "Sameera just moved here from Saudi Arabia with her family," said Miss Murphy. "I'll introduce you to her." She looked at all the students seated in front of her. "If I can find her . . ." She turned to scan the rest of the room. A black-haired girl was kneeling by the guinea pig's cage. It was the same black-haired girl Jenny had seen on the playground, yelling at the boys.

"Sameera," said the teacher, raising her voice. "Come here." Slowly Sameera walked toward them. "This is Jenny," said Miss Murphy, nodding toward Jenny. "She's been writing mouse letters to you."

Sameera looked at Jenny. Her face had no expression at all. Her dark-brown eyes seemed to look right through Jenny. Then she looked away.

"Jenny, maybe you could read to Sameera," said Miss Murphy.

Uh-oh. The teacher had come up with a plan to have them be friends. Jenny didn't like this plan at all.

"I'll check with your teacher and see if you can come back tomorrow morning," the teacher continued. "That would be so nice." She smiled at Jenny.

Jenny nodded, but she really didn't think that would be nice at all. Sameera didn't seem very friendly.

Chapter 5

The next morning Mrs. Steele called Jenny to her desk during silent reading time. "I talked to Miss Murphy yesterday. She would like you to read to Sameera. That way you could get to know each other."

Jenny nodded slowly. She wasn't sure she wanted to get to know Sameera.

"Why don't you go to the second-grade classroom and see if this is a good time?" said Mrs. Steele.

Jenny hoped it wasn't a good time. She walked down the hall, pausing to look at the animal pictures on the bulletin board. She drank from the water fountain. She stopped in the girls' bathroom. When she finally reached Miss Murphy's room, she stood in the doorway. One group of children was reading to the teacher. Another group sat at a table with paintbrushes and colorful, autumn leaves.

Miss Murphy looked up and saw Jenny. "Sameera is helping me teach leaf printing this morning," she said. "She did such a good job on her leaf print yesterday." Miss Murphy walked over to the table that held colorful autumn leaves, paint, and papers. She motioned for Jenny to join her.

"I don't know what to do," said a boy with glasses.

"Sameera, are you showing them how to do it?" said Miss Murphy. "Come show Daniel."

Daniel picked up a brush, dipped it in green paint, and started to paint the paper in front of him.

"No, no, no," said Sameera, grabbing his brush. She painted the leaf. Then she placed a piece of white paper on top of the leaf and pressed on the paper with a roller.

"What's she doing?" asked Daniel.

Sameera said some funny words and pulled the paper off the leaf.

"Pretty," said Daniel, pointing to the imprint of the leaf on the white paper.

"Let me see," said a boy who was wearing a red shirt. He grabbed the paper.

"No," said Sameera, grabbing the leaf print back.

"Eric, you're not wearing a paint smock," said Miss Murphy. "Please put one on."

Eric frowned. He was holding a sponge. He tossed it toward Sameera. It landed on her paper.

Sameera yelled angrily at him, *"Koobla-koo-ya."* To Jenny it sounded like a witch's chant. She wondered if Eric would suddenly turn into a toad.

"Sameera," said Miss Murphy in a firm voice. "Stop that."

Sameera looked up at Miss Murphy and said, *"Ricki-ka-bob."* Perhaps the teacher would turn into a hippo. A hippo with wire-rimmed glasses.

"Sameera, please speak English," said Miss Murphy.

Suddenly it all made sense. Sameera couldn't speak English. No wonder she couldn't write letters.

Miss Murphy put her arm around Jenny and drew her closer to the table. "Sameera, Jenny is going to read to you."

Sameera looked up. Then she looked away. Jenny wondered if she understood what Miss Murphy had said. Did she have any idea who Jenny was? Sameera gave Daniel fresh paper and a new leaf.

"Sameera, you can finish leaf painting later," said Miss Murphy.

"No," said Sameera. "Paint."

Miss Murphy looked at the clock. "Let's see. The children have music class in fifteen minutes. That's not much time. Can you come back tomorrow at nine-fifteen?"

Jenny shrugged, "I guess so."

"Sameera, Jenny will come back tomorrow and read to you," said Miss Murphy.

Sameera gave Miss Murphy a blank stare.

No doubt about it. Sameera was not thrilled to hear that Jenny would be back.

"I have some easier books here," said Miss Murphy, leading Jenny over to her desk. "Or you could bring a book. Sameera can understand some English, but she often speaks in Arabic. I think you could help Sameera a lot."

Jenny tried to smile. She looked back over at Sameera before she left the room. Sameera picked up a leaf and Eric grabbed it from her hand. She yelled at him, *"Rick-poo-dah!"*

Jenny hurried out the door. Why did she have to get stuck with Sameera! She wanted a new pen pal—a normal person who could speak and write English.

Chapter 6

When Jenny returned to her own classroom, Mrs. Steele was explaining adjectives. "An adjective is a helping word. It tells something about a noun."

Jenny slipped quickly into her seat.

"You're *so* late," Susan hissed.

Jenny ignored her.

Kevin leaned over and wrote on Mary's back with the end of his pen.

"Stop that, Kevin," said Mary. She looked over her shoulder and tried to see the back of her shirt.

"It's okay," whispered Jenny. "He wasn't using the inky end."

"Kevin, what is a noun?" said Mrs. Steele.

"A snake is a noun," he said.

Jenny stared at him. He had his snake shirt on again. It had grass stains on the back.

"Yes, the word 'snake' is a noun," said Mrs. Steele. "What other words are nouns?"

Kevin shrugged.

"A noun is a person, place, or thing," said Susan.

"Yes," said Mrs. Steele. "That's exactly right."

Mrs. Steele wrote a sentence on the board. "The young man sat on the bench," she read. "Which word is an adjective?"

"Young," said Mary.

"Right," said Mrs. Steele. "Now change the sentence and use another adjective."

"The old man sat on the green bench," said Susan.

"Very good," said Mrs. Steele. "You used two adjectives—old and green. Can someone else change the sentence?"

"The green man sat on the old bench," said Richard.

Mrs. Steele laughed. "Good, Richard. Now, class, I want you to write another mouse letter, using lots of adjectives."

"The green mouse sat on the old bench," said Richard.

Everyone laughed.

"We only have a short time before P.E.," said Mrs. Steele. "See how many adjectives you can use."

Jenny stared at the blank sheet of paper on her desk. She had no idea what to write. She didn't see any reason to write mouse letters to a girl who couldn't read them or write back. Sameera seemed so unfriendly. Unfriendly Sameera. Unfriendly was an adjective. Jenny was not looking forward to reading books to unfriendly Sameera tomorrow. She sighed and looked at her blank sheet of paper. She drew a picture of a mouse. Next to his mouth, she drew a balloon like the comic strips have. In the balloon she wrote, "Chocolate brownies!" Brownie was the name of a thing. Chocolate must be an adjective. A very tasty adjective.

Next she drew a picture of a dog with a mouse on its back. The mouse said, "Run faster." No adjective there. She added another sentence. "The black dog is going to catch us." Black was another adjective. She had two adjectives, but no letter.

"Pass your letters to the front of the room," said Mrs. Steele.

Jenny didn't have anything to hand in. Mary turned around and held out her hand for Jenny's letter. Jenny quickly wrote, "Dear Sameera," at the top of the letter and, "Sincerely, Whiskers," at the bottom.

"Hurry up," said Mary.

Jenny made a face at Mary. Then she turned around to get Richard's letter. He put his letter on Jenny's head. It floated to the floor. Jenny picked it up. She noticed it was very short. She placed his letter on top of hers and passed them both to Mary.

"I liked your picture letter," said Richard.

"You did?" said Jenny.

"You're good at drawing," said Richard.

Jenny could feel her face getting red. She didn't know what to say to Richard.

"Your pictures are so informative." He pursed his lips and fluttered his eyelashes as he said it.

"You're making fun of me," said Jenny.

"No way," said Richard. "I wouldn't make fun of you. I'm making fun of someone else." He nodded toward Susan. "I really think your pictures are good."

Jenny smiled at Richard.

Chapter 7

The next morning Jenny entered the second-grade classroom, clutching two books to her chest. She had brought them from home. They were two of her favorites: *Alexander and the Wind-up Mouse* and *If You Give a Mouse a Cookie.* The pages were worn from frequent reading.

Jenny walked over to Miss Murphy's desk and waited for the teacher to notice her. Miss Murphy was reading a student's paper and making marks on it with a red pen.

Sameera stood by the coat closet. Jenny watched as Sameera opened the closet door and peered inside. Sameera closed the door and stood between two desks. She put one hand on one desk, one hand on the other, and swung between the desks. Next she picked up a yardstick and looked at it closely before putting it down. Then she walked sideways toward the class-room door, never taking her eyes off Miss Murphy.

"Eric," said Miss Murphy. "Here's your paper. You forgot to answer the last question." She handed the paper to Eric. Finally she noticed Jenny. "Oh, good, you've brought some books for Sameera." Miss Murphy looked around the room. Jenny looked, too. Sameera had disappeared.

"Has anyone seen Sameera?" said Miss Murphy.

"She was standing near the door a minute ago," said Daniel, grinning. Daniel wore glasses with silver frames. He looked like a little professor.

"Oh, dear," said Miss Murphy. She got up, walked to the door, and looked up and down the hall.

"She disappears a lot," Daniel told Jenny. He looked at her over the top of his glasses like her grandfather did. Daniel seemed like a grown-up stuck in a kid's small body.

A voice boomed over the intercom. "Miss Murphy," the voice said. It was the principal. "Sameera just walked by the office."

"This happens all the time," said Daniel.

"Jenny," said Miss Murphy, "would you mind going to the office to get Sameera? Bring her back to the room."

That was the last thing Jenny wanted to do. "Do you think Sameera will come with me?" Jenny asked.

"Just take her by the hand," said Miss Murphy. "She'll come back."

Jenny hesitated.

"Hurry," said Miss Murphy. "We don't want her to leave the building."

"I'll go," said Daniel.

"You have work to do at your desk, Daniel," said Miss Murphy, sternly.

Jenny hurried toward the office. She imagined chasing Sameera down the streets of the neighborhood. "I'm not going to hurt you, Sameera," she would yell. "I'm just going to read mouse books to you."

Jenny didn't see Sameera by the office. She turned the corner. Sameera was standing by the library. She looked up as Jenny came toward her, her face blank.

Jenny stood next to her. "Sameera, I'm Jenny. I'm supposed to read to you."

Sameera stared at Jenny.

"Come," said Jenny. She held out her hand.

Sameera held Jenny's hand. She didn't smile, but she didn't run away. Jenny felt relieved. She led Sameera back to the classroom.

Miss Murphy looked up when Jenny entered the classroom with Sameera, but then turned back to the student she was helping. Jenny guessed she was on her own with Sameera.

"I have some books," Jenny said. She still had the books clutched in her other hand. She held them out for Sameera to see. Sameera looked away.

"Where can we read?" asked Jenny as she looked around the room. A red-and-blue plaid couch stood against the wall. Jenny led Sameera to the couch and sat down. Sameera hesitated. Then she sat down, too.

Jenny opened the first book. She took a deep breath and started to read. She pointed to the mouse and said his name. Jenny tilted the book so Sameera could see the picture. She read slowly. The book had some hard words. She stumbled on the words "pebble path." She had to sound out the word "quivering."

When Jenny read the last page of the book, she said, "The end." She closed the book.

Sameera didn't say anything.

"Did you like the book?" Jenny asked.

Sameera nodded.

"Should I read another book?" Jenny asked.

Sameera shrugged.

Jenny guessed that meant Sameera didn't care one way or another. At least she sat on the couch and listened. Well, maybe she wasn't listening, but at least she sat still. She didn't leave the room. Jenny looked over at Miss Murphy. Miss Murphy looked up and smiled at her and nodded her head. Jenny figured the teacher was encouraging her to go ahead and read more. She opened the second book. It was about a mouse who ate a cookie. When she said the word "cookie," Jenny pretended she was eating a cookie and said, "Yum, yum."

Sameera grinned.

Jenny smiled back. It was the first time she had seen Sameera look happy. She read on. Sameera didn't grin again, but she held one side of the book and seemed to be paying attention.

The recess bell rang. All the kids rushed for their coats.

Jenny was in the middle of reading the last page of the book.

Sameera jumped up. Without a backward look, she rushed to get her coat and left the room.

Jenny watched her go.

Chapter 8

Jenny went back to her classroom to get her coat. She put the books inside her desk.

When she came in from recess, Mrs. Steele had a book in her hand. It was a thick one. Jenny liked books with lots of pictures best. This didn't look like a picture book.

"Everyone come up and sit on the floor," said Mrs. Steele. "I'm going to read to you."

Chairs scraped. Jenny followed her classmates to the front of the room.

"Sit on the carpet," said Mrs. Steele, "and all eyes look at me."

Jenny liked looking at her teacher. Today she had on her Mrs. Farmer outfit—denim skirt, a red shirt, and a red-checkered scarf around her neck.

"Richard, you're not sitting," said Mrs. Steele.

Richard had been lying down. He sat up.

"This book is called *Stuart Little* by E. B. White," said Mrs. Steele.

"What kind of name is Eeebee?" asked Richard.

"Those are his initials," said Mrs. Steele.

"What do they stand for?" asked Kevin.

"I don't know," said Mrs. Steele. She opened the book and started to read.

"Maybe the author's name is something embarrassing, like 'Egbert,' " said Richard.

"Egbert Bozo," said Jenny.

Mrs. Steele cleared her throat. She glared at Jenny and Richard. "If you talk, you won't be able to hear the story."

Jenny was embarrassed. She looked down at her shoes. A glob of mud was stuck on one side. She picked at it with her finger. Now there was dirt under her nail.

Mrs. Steele started to read again. The story was about a baby who was very tiny when he was born. His name was Stuart and he was the size of a mouse. He even looked like a mouse.

Yuck. Jenny was tired of mice. She was also uncomfortable, squeezed between Kevin and Susan. She moved back a little and crossed her legs.

Richard raised his hand. "This isn't real, is it?" he asked. "People can't have mice for children, can they?"

"No," said Mrs. Steele. "This is a fantasy just like your mouse letters to the second graders."

Jenny thought about Sameera. Jenny had really tried to write good letters. And she had picked her favorite mouse books to read to Sameera. But Sameera didn't seem interested in mouse stories. Or else she couldn't understand them. Jenny picked at the mud on her shoe again.

Mrs. Steele read how Stuart's father made him a tiny bed out of four clothespins and a little box. When Stuart was a week old, he could climb lamp cords. That sounded like fun.

Jenny stopped picking at the mud. She moved her foot so Mrs. Steele wouldn't see the small pile of dirt from her shoe.

Stuart the mouse had lots of adventures. He slid down the dark and slimy bathtub drain to find his mother's ring. He climbed inside the piano to fix a sticking key. He found Ping-Pong balls under the sofa.

Mrs. Steele shut the book and laid it in her lap.

"Aw," said Richard. "Read some more."

"I'll read more tomorrow," said Mrs. Steele. "You must like the story, Richard."

"I want to find out what's in the mouse hole,"

said Richard. "The one Stuart's father doesn't want Stuart to wander into."

Mrs. Steele raised her eyebrows and nodded. "Yes, that is intriguing."

"Intriguing?" said Jenny.

"That means interesting," said know-it-all Susan.

"What else did you like about the story?" asked Mrs. Steele.

"This has given me ideas for my next mouse letter," said Susan.

"Good," said Mrs. Steele. "I hoped it would. And speaking of mouse letters, I have some to hand back to you." She opened a big envelope, took out a stack of papers, and passed them out.

Jenny knew she wouldn't get a letter. She wished she wasn't sitting right next to Susan. Susan would notice when Mrs. Steele didn't deliver a letter to her.

Mrs. Steele looked at the clock. "It's eleven-forty," she said. "We have time to read one letter before lunch."

Susan's hand shot up.

"Susan," said Mrs. Steele. "Share your letter with us."

"Dear Pepper Jack," Susan read. "Why don't you

like rats?" Susan stopped. She looked up at the class. "In my last letter, I told Daniel I didn't like rats because they are smelly and carry diseases." She said it like she was an expert on rats.

Jenny didn't think pet rats had diseases. And they probably weren't smelly if you cleaned their cages.

Susan continued reading the letter from Daniel.

"I like rats. Rats look like mice, only they're bigger. They have long tails and pointy faces and whiskers. My friend really likes his pet rat. Ratface sits on his shoulder. Ratface sat on my shoulder once. Maybe you don't know any rats, so you think they're bad.
                Sincerely,
                Daniel"

Susan held up Daniel's paper. "He wrote a very long letter to me. See how neatly he writes. I made this stationery and gave it to him."

"That *is* a long letter," said Mrs. Steele. "And I like the nice stationery you created." She took the

letter from Susan and held it up for everyone to see.

"I wanted to help him write good letters," said Susan. "I showed him where to write the date and the greeting and the complimentary close. I made lots of lines for the body. He filled in all the lines with his writing."

"Very nice, Susan," said Mrs. Steele, handing back her letter. "Now it's time to line up for lunch. Put your letters inside your desks first."

Jenny stood up and hurried to her desk. She was glad she didn't have to hear Susan brag anymore about her great letters.

But Susan followed her. "You didn't get a letter, did you?"

"No," said Jenny.

"What's wrong with your second grader?" asked Susan.

"I don't think she can write very well," said Jenny.

"You should make her some stationery like this." Susan held out her letter.

"I don't think that would help," said Jenny. "She doesn't speak English."

"Oh," said Susan. "Well, it still might help."

"I don't know," said Jenny. "I don't know if anything will help."

Chapter 9

After school, Jenny thought about Sameera for a long time. She thought about her while she was walking home. She thought about her while she was eating her snack. She thought about her while she watched television and played with her little brother. Toby was only two years old and he didn't speak much English, but Jenny usually knew what he wanted. Right now he wanted help with his circus train. She hooked the engine and the other cars together and helped him put the animals on the train. Toby made *choo-choo* noises as he pushed the train around the room.

Maybe Jenny could help Sameera write a letter. Maybe the stationery idea wasn't so bad after all.

Jenny got some plain white paper, a ruler, and a pencil. She drew a line at the top of the paper and wrote "Date" beside it. She would show Sameera

how to write the date. For the greeting, she wrote, "Dear Whiskers." The body of the letter would be the hardest part. Maybe she could write questions. Then all Sameera would have to do was answer them.

Toby climbed on the chair beside her. He reached for her pencil. She let him take it. She put a blank sheet of paper in front of him. He tried to scribble on her letter, but she held it in the air. "No, Toby, write on *your* paper," she said.

"No," he said, but scribbled all over his paper anyway. Then he climbed down, dropped the pencil under the table, and went back to his train.

"Thanks, Toby," Jenny said, as she crawled under the table to get her pencil. She sat at the table again and thought about questions she could ask Sameera. Sameera knew the word "no" just like Toby did. And she used it a lot just like Toby. She probably knew "yes" as well. Jenny could write questions where the answer was "yes" or "no."

"Do you have any brothers?" Jenny wrote. "Do you have any sisters?" She drew a line after each question where Sameera could write "yes" or "no."

She needed more questions to fill the paper. She could ask questions about Saudi Arabia. "Was your school in Saudi Arabia like our school?" she wrote.

What else could she ask about? "Did you live in a city?" "Do you have a bicycle?" "Do you play sports?" These were all good questions.

Munchkin the cat jumped into Jenny's lap. "Do you have cats and dogs?" Jenny wrote. "Do you have mice?"

Now the letter looked very long. It looked just as long as Susan's letter.

On Monday morning, Jenny went to the second-grade classroom with her letter full of questions. Sameera was standing by the teacher's desk.

"Jenny," said Miss Murphy. "I'm glad you're here. Why don't you read to Sameera in the library today?"

Jenny led Sameera to the library and sat down at a table.

Sameera didn't sit down. She said, "Book," and pointed to the picture book shelves. Jenny got up and followed her. "We can read one book," Jenny said, "and then I'll show you how to write a letter."

Sameera picked out three books and handed them to Jenny. Jenny read one of the books to Sameera. Then she picked up the paper she had worked on so hard the day before. "This is a letter," Jenny said. "I will show you what to write."

Sameera looked at the paper. Then she picked up another book.

"Yes," said Jenny, taking the book, "I will read that in a minute. But first I will help you write a letter." She handed Sameera a pencil. "You write the date here."

Sameera held the pencil, but she didn't write anything.

"I'll show you what to write," said Jenny. "October 23," Jenny wrote on a blank piece of paper. "Now write that here," and she pointed to the line on the letter.

Sameera pointed to the date Jenny had written. "In Saudi Arabia . . . umm . . . different."

"What's different?" asked Jenny.

"Umm . . . too hard," said Sameera. "I ask Mother."

One of Sameera's classmates hurried over to their table. "Sameera, you have to go to E.S.L. now," she said. "The teacher is waiting."

Sameera grabbed the questions and left. She didn't say good-bye.

Jenny walked slowly back to her classroom. She wasn't sure what E.S.L. meant. Maybe the letters stood for Eat, Swing, and Leap.

Jenny stood by the teacher's desk. Mrs. Steele was wearing her pumpkin sweater. It was black with large orange pumpkins and a scarecrow.

"Sameera had to go somewhere," Jenny told her teacher. "E.S.L.?"

"Oh, yes," said Mrs. Steele. "English as a Second Language. It's a class to help her speak English better."

"Oh," said Jenny.

Mrs. Steele handed her a paper with math problems on it. "We've been doing math groups," she said. "These are division problems like we've had all week. Susan's been working hard on them. Have her help you."

Oh, goody, thought Jenny. She sat down next to Susan and looked at the problems.

"Share three cookies equally among four people," the first problem said. "Put each person's share in a box. How much does each person eat?"

That was a hard problem. Jenny looked at Susan's paper. "How did you get three fourths?" Jenny asked.

"Where were you all this time?" asked Susan.

Jenny didn't answer.

"Well?" said Susan.

"I was doing something else," said Jenny.

Susan frowned. She drew three cookies. "First I divided each cookie in half, but that only gave me six pieces," she said. "I couldn't share them equally with four people."

"Give me all the cookies," said Richard. "Then the problem goes away."

Jenny laughed.

Susan ignored Richard. She drew three cookies again. "Next I divided each cookie into thirds. But that didn't work, either."

"I get it now," said Jenny. "When you divide each cookie into four pieces, you get twelve pieces in all. So each person gets three pieces."

"That's right," said Susan, looking very pleased.

Jenny was pleased, too. She was glad Susan had to work hard to figure out the answer. Jenny had always thought Susan knew all the answers without doing any work. Using cookies was a good way to explain math. Jenny wished she had a real cookie. She was glad it was almost lunchtime.

After lunch, when the rest of the class went out for recess, Jenny returned to her classroom. Mrs. Steele looked up when she came in. "How did it go with Sameera this morning?"

Jenny stood close to the teacher's desk. "I read her a book," she said.

"And did she like the story?" asked Mrs. Steele.

"I couldn't tell," said Jenny. "She didn't say anything. Then I tried to help her write a letter, but she had trouble with the date."

"Oh," said Mrs. Steele.

"I don't think . . . " Jenny hesitated. "I don't think Sameera will ever write me a letter."

"I talked to Miss Murphy last night. She thinks Sameera can understand some English, but she's too shy to speak much." Mrs. Steele paused. "What do you think?"

"She doesn't seem shy when she yells at the boys," said Jenny.

"Miss Murphy thinks the boys are mean to Sameera."

"It's so hard to talk to her," said Jenny. "Can I . . . have a different student?"

"I know you must be feeling very discouraged," said Mrs. Steele. "But I think you should try again. Sometimes a hard job is a gift."

A gift! How could a job be a gift? How could helping Sameera be a gift? Jenny looked down at the floor. She pictured Sameera with a big red bow around her. If Sameera was a gift, then it was like the gift Great-aunt Hazel gave her for her birthday—an itchy sweater she couldn't wear. She had hidden the sweater on the floor of her closet.

"Will you try again?" asked Mrs. Steele. "I think Sameera needs a friend."

Jenny looked up at her teacher. She wanted to please Mrs. Steele. "I'll try," she said.

Chapter 10

Jenny crunched through fallen leaves on her way home from school. A gust of wind blew more leaves onto the sidewalk. The trees still had some orange leaves on them, but not too many. Soon they would be bare and winter would come. Jenny wondered if Sameera celebrated Christmas in Saudi Arabia. Maybe she could ask her. But how? Maybe Jenny could read her a Christmas book. But Jenny was tired of reading to Sameera, because she sat like a big, stuffed doll who didn't understand anything.

Mrs. Steele had said a hard job was a gift. Sameera was a gift Jenny wanted to take back to the store and exchange. Who would Jenny rather have? Daniel wrote good letters to Susan. Jenny would take Daniel.

Jenny thought about Christmas some more. She loved making Christmas cookies. She decided to make some cookies that afternoon. She could use the cookies to help with the math worksheet she hadn't finished in class. Then she could eat all the cookie pieces when she had done the problems.

When Jenny got home, her mother helped her find a recipe for sugar cookies. Jenny looked through the drawer where they kept the cookie cutters. The Christmas ones were on top—a big tree, a star, an angel, a gingerbread man. There were lots of animals, too. Plain round circles would probably be easiest for math problems. But she would make some more interesting cookies as well. Jenny picked out an elephant, a giraffe, a bear, and a tiger. She wished she had a mouse cookie cutter. Suddenly she had a wonderful idea. She would make mouse cookies for Sameera and act out stories with them. Maybe that would make Sameera smile and pay attention.

"Mom, we have to go to the store and find a mouse cookie cutter," said Jenny.

"We can't go now," said her mother, "because Toby is sleeping. Why don't you design your own mouse cookie? You can make a pattern out of cardboard, then cut around it with a knife."

"A cookie cutter would be easier," said Jenny.

"I know," said her mother. "But easy isn't always better. Think how creative you can be. You can

make the mouse look exactly like you want him to look. Then you can decorate him with frosting."

"Will you help me?" asked Jenny.

"Sure," said her mother. "You draw the mouse. Draw lots of mice. Different sizes, different shapes. We can experiment and see which one turns out the best."

Jenny sighed and went to find some paper. First she drew a mouse standing up like a person. She gave him big ears. It looked like a teddy bear. He needed a tail. She drew a long thin tail.

"Look at this mouse," said Jenny.

"I like him," said her mother. "But his skinny tail might be hard to cut out of dough."

Jenny made the tail thicker. Now the mouse looked like a kangaroo. Next she drew a mouse running along the ground, with a sausage-shaped body and a pointy nose and a short, thin tail. She looked through some mouse books. She drew more mouse bodies.

"Great mice!" said her mother. She helped Jenny cut them out. Some of the tails fell off when the mice were moved to the cookie sheet. Jenny pressed them back with her thumb.

"I like this one best," said Jenny. It was a mouse with a face like a triangle.

"Good. We'll make lots of that one," said her mother.

Soon the cookie tray was full of mice.

"I'm going to act out my mouse letters with the cookies," said Jenny. "I'll take my plastic tea set, because I wrote about mice eating and drinking coffee."

"Drinking coffee?" said her mother. "Sophisticated mice."

"They steal it from the teachers' lounge," said Jenny. "I'll bring some furniture from my dollhouse, too."

Jenny was getting excited now. She was sure Sameera would like her mouse cookies. "If only Sameera would write me a letter," said Jenny.

"Help her write one," said her mother.

"I tried that already," said Jenny. "We got stuck on the date. She said something about the date being different."

"I think they use a different calendar," said her mother.

"Really?" said Jenny.

"Get the encyclopedia and look it up," said her mother.

"I don't want to look it up," said Jenny. "I want Sameera to tell me about it in a letter."

Her mother left the room and returned with volume C of the encyclopedia. "Listen to this," said her mother. "The Islamic calendar starts from the year A.D. 622. That was the year Mohammed left Mecca for Medina."

"Who was Mohammed?" said Jenny. "What does 'A.D.' mean?"

Just then Toby walked in, rubbing his eyes. He pushed a chair to the counter, climbed up, and grabbed an unbaked cookie.

"Stop him, Mom!" wailed Jenny. "He's ruining everything." She held the cookie tray out of Toby's reach.

Her mother picked Toby up and put him on her hip. With her free hand, she held the encyclopedia out to Jenny. "Read about the Gregorian calendar. That is the one we use," she said.

"Mom, I'm busy!" said Jenny. She put the cookie pan in the oven.

Her mother read, "Our calendar is based on the year Jesus Christ was born. Dates after his birth are written as A.D., which means, 'in the year of the Lord.' "

Toby screamed and tried to grab the encyclopedia. Jenny's mother put the book down and got a box of cookies from the pantry. She put Toby on the floor and handed him two cookies. "Mohammed is the man who started the Islamic religion," Jenny's mother said.

"No wonder Sameera couldn't explain it to me," said Jenny.

"You're learning interesting new things from Sameera," said her mother.

"I'm learning interesting things from the encyclopedia," said Jenny.

Chapter 11

Jenny took the cookies to school the next day in a tin. She left her classroom during reading groups to meet Sameera. They sat at Sameera's desk.

"I am going to tell you about the mouse who writes my letters," she said. "And I have cookies. I will tell the story with cookies."

Sameera looked puzzled.

Jenny opened the cookie tin. "These are mouse cookies." She took a mouse from the tin. "This is Whiskers. He is the mouse who lives in your desk."

"Whis-kers," said Sameera.

Jenny nodded. She got a doll bed out of a plastic bag. "Bed," she said. "Put Whiskers to bed." She put the mouse cookie on the bed. "Now we will put him in your desk." She put the bed with the mouse inside Sameera's desk. "Mouse in desk," she said.

"Mouse in desk," said Sameera and she giggled. "Whiskers in bed."

Jenny's idea was working. She got the four brothers out of the cookie tin. "These are the brothers—Moe, Max, Sam, and Joe. I wrote their names in icing." She held each one up and said his name.

One of Sameera's classmates stood by the desk and watched.

"Should we put Moe to bed?" asked Jenny.

Sameera picked up the Moe cookie. "Eat Moe," she said and made biting motions with her mouth.

"You want to eat Moe?" said Jenny. She made her voice sound horrified, but she could not help laughing.

"Yes," said Sameera.

"Okay," said Jenny. "Eat Moe. I'll eat Max. Bite his head off." And she bit off his head.

Sameera bit off Moe's head.

"Next his tail," said Jenny.

"Tail?" said Sameera.

"This is the tail," said Jenny, pointing to Moe's tail.

Sameera bit off the tail.

"And now the body," said Jenny. And she popped the rest of Max the Mouse into her mouth.

Sameera did the same thing and they both laughed.

By now, several students stood by Sameera's desk.

"Daniel, Eric," said Miss Murphy. "Where are our books? You're supposed to be reading."

"This is more fun," said Daniel. "I want to eat a mouse."

More students crowded around Sameera's desk.

Daniel grabbed a cookie. Sameera slapped his hand, but Daniel ate Sam. Eric grabbed Joe.

"No, no," yelled Sameera.

"It's okay," said Jenny. "We still have Whiskers. He is safe inside the desk."

Sameera reached inside the desk. "Here is Whiskers." She set the mouse bed on her desk.

"Don't eat Whiskers," Jenny told the boys.

Miss Murphy was standing by Sameera's desk. "A mouse cookie. What a clever idea," she said.

"Whiskers is the mouse who writes letters," said Jenny.

Sameera bent down and reached inside the desk again. "Letter."

Jenny took the paper from Sameera. It was her list of questions. Someone had written answers on the paper.

"Mother help me," said Sameera.

Jenny was surprised that Sameera had bothered to take the questions home. It wasn't a proper letter from Sameera. But it was a step in the right direction.

"The date is funny," said Daniel. He pointed to the date and stared at Jenny over the top of his glasses.

"Twenty-five Rajab, 1421," Jenny read. "In Saudi Arabia, they use the Islamic calendar. It's different from our calendar."

"Cool," said Daniel.

Jenny read the first question. "Do you have any brothers?" Then she read the answer. "Yes."

"How many?" said Daniel.

"How many brothers?" Jenny asked Sameera. Jenny held up one finger. "One brother?"

"Yes," said Sameera, nodding. "One brother." She held up one finger.

Jenny read the next question. "Do you have any sisters?" She read the answer. "Yes."

Sameera held up two fingers.

"Two sisters," said Daniel.

Jenny read another question. "Was your school in Saudi Arabia like our school?" Jenny stopped.

The answer was not "yes" or "no." Sameera's mother had written a longer answer. "Boys and girls never go to the same school in Saudi Arabia," Jenny read. "They go to separate schools."

"No boys at your school?" said Daniel. "How awful!"

Everyone laughed. Even Sameera laughed.

"Read some more," said Eric.

"Did you live in a city?" Jenny read. "Yes, in Jedda."

"Jedda," said Miss Murphy. "Let's look for that on the map." She walked to the blackboard and pulled down the world map. The children crowded around her. "Sameera, let's show the class where you lived." Miss Murphy pointed to Jedda.

Sameera stood beside the teacher. She pointed where the teacher was pointing.

The recess bell rang. "Everyone get your coats," said Miss Murphy.

Sameera stayed with Jenny while she packed up her plastic bed and dishes.

"You can keep Whiskers," Jenny said.

"I like Whiskers," said Sameera. "I keep him."

Jenny gave her the cookie tin, and Sameera put the mouse cookie inside.

"Thank you for sharing with the class, Jenny," said Miss Murphy.

Jenny practically floated back to her classroom. Everyone had liked her cookie mice. Especially Sameera. That was the best part.

Chapter 12

The next morning Jenny spotted Sameera right away on the playground. She was holding a ball and yelling at several boys. "No, no. Mine! It's mine!" she screamed.

Eric walked over, and Jenny watched him talk to Sameera. Finally she handed him the ball. He put the ball down, and in slow motion, gave it a kick. One of the boys brought the ball back and Sameera kicked the ball. It didn't go very far. Without kicking the ball again, Eric showed Sameera how to swing her leg back and bring it forward. "See," he said.

Richard walked up to Jenny. "Is that your pen pal?" he asked.

Jenny nodded. "She's sort of a pen pal. I write letters to her. She doesn't write back. Not yet anyway."

"Sort of a pal without a pen," said Richard.

Just then, Sameera gave the ball a mighty wallop. It hit Daniel in the stomach. His glasses flew off and landed in the dirt. He bent over as the ball shot back toward Sameera. Everyone stopped and looked at Daniel. He squinted at Sameera in surprise. "Good kick," he said.

"I taught her to do that," said Eric.

Sameera walked over to Daniel, picked up his glasses, blew them off, and handed them back to him.

"Thank you very much," said Daniel.

The bell rang, signaling the end of recess. Richard and Jenny walked toward their classroom. "Did you notice that she didn't yell at the boys in Arabic?" said Jenny. "She yelled at them in English. Isn't that great?"

Mrs. Steele stood in front of the class, holding some papers. She waited for everyone to sit down. Jenny watched as Mrs. Steele adjusted one of her puffy sleeves. She was wearing her Bo-Peep dress. It was Jenny's favorite. The dress had pink-and-white stripes and a full skirt. "I have some letters from the second graders," Mrs. Steele said.

"Already?" said Kevin. "We just wrote them."

Jenny didn't let herself hope that there would be a letter for her. At least she had gotten a letter from Sameera's mother. It was better than her usual nothing.

"The first one is for Whiskers," said Mrs. Steele.

Jenny couldn't believe it. She walked to the front of the room with her heart pounding. Her hands trembled as she took the letter from Mrs. Steele. Jenny read slowly, not sure what to expect. "Dear Whiskers," she read. "I liked your mouse cookies. They made Sameera laugh. She even talked." Jenny stopped and found herself smiling, too. "Sincerely, Eric."

So Sameera hadn't written to her, but Eric had!

"The next one is from Daniel," said Mrs. Steele.

"That's my student," said Susan. She put out her hand.

"It's not for you, Susan," said Mrs. Steele. "It's for Whiskers."

"For Whiskers?" Susan seemed stunned.

Mrs. Steele winked as she handed Jenny the letter.

Jenny took the letter, but stole a glance at Susan before reading it. Susan was looking down at her desk. Jenny couldn't believe that Susan's prize pen pal was writing her. She was pleased but slightly embarrassed, too.

"Go ahead. Read it," said Mrs. Steele.

"Dear Whiskers," Jenny read. "It was fun to learn about Sameera's school. I was surprised that boys and girls don't go to school together. I didn't know about the Islamic calendar. That was very interesting. The cookies were a great idea. I liked eating Sam. He tasted good. Sincerely, Daniel."

"He liked eating Sam?" said Richard. "Is this guy a cannibal or what?"

"He's *my* pen pal," said Susan, sounding very annoyed.

"That explains it," said Richard.

"Sam was a mouse cookie, not a person," explained Jenny. "Daniel wrote a P.S., too."

"Who else did he eat?" asked Richard.

"He didn't eat anybody," said Jenny. "He wrote, 'Sameera needed some help today. I helped her.'" Jenny could picture the little professor helping Sameera and peering at her over his glasses. His glasses that were now dusty.

"The rest of the letters are for Whiskers, too," said Mrs. Steele, leafing through them. "Tell us about the mouse cookies and Sameera. You obviously made a big impression on the whole class."

So Jenny told them about using the mouse cookies to act out a story about Whiskers.

"What a great idea!" said Mrs. Steele. "Good job, Jenny."

Jenny glowed.

"Great letters," Richard said as Jenny sat down. "But you forgot to give *me* a mouse cookie."

"I can make you some," said Jenny.

"Teach us all how to make mouse cookies," said Mary.

"Yes," said Susan. "I want to make a mouse cookie for Daniel."

"Would you like to do that, Jenny?" asked Mrs. Steele.

Jenny nodded happily.

"Bring me your recipe tomorrow and we can plan a cookie day for Friday," said Mrs. Steele. "We can make the cookies in the classroom. Jenny can show everyone how to do it. Then during recess, Jenny and I can bake the cookies in the teachers' lounge."

Jenny couldn't believe it. She'd spend her recess in the teachers' lounge with her favorite teacher. Maybe Mrs. Steele would even wear her Bo-Peep dress again with a frilly apron.

"And I'll help taste the cookies," said Richard. "I'm good at that."

Jenny giggled. "We'll make a mouse cookie for each of our pen pals." She turned to Richard. "And for everyone in our class, too."

"I can't wait!" said Richard.

"Oh, Jenny," said Mrs. Steele as she started to hand her the stack of letters. "Would you read us one more letter? This is a special one." She placed the special letter on top of the stack.

Jenny looked at the letter for a minute. Over the lump of happiness in her throat, she read,

"Dear Whiskers,
I have a mouse in my desk.
I like him.
My frend Jenny made him."

The letter was signed, "Sameera."